Little
Red Ink
Drinker

OTHER DELL YEARLING BOOKS YOU WILL ENJOY

Little Red Ink Drinker

story by ÉRIC SANVOISIN
illustrations by MARTIN MATJE

LE PETIT BUVEUR D'ENCRE ROUGE
translated by GEORGES MOROZ

A Dell Yearling Book

Published by
Dell Yearling
an imprint of
Random House Children's Books
a division of Random House, Inc.
New York

First American Edition 2003
Originally published by Les Éditions Nathan, Paris, 2002

Visit us on the Web! www.randomhouse.com/kids

Educators and librarians, for a variety of teaching tools, visit us at
www.randomhouse.com/teachers

ISBN: 0-440-41845-3

Reprinted by arrangement with Delacorte Press

Printed in the United States of America

July 2004

10 9 8 7 6 5 4 3 2 1

For Awena, the little #8
—E.S.

For Gérard D.
—M.M.

one

Once Upon a Time, There Was . . . Dracuville!

Odilon is my name. Before my encounter with Draculink, the ink drinker, I was an ordinary boy. But one day the old vampire bit me—even though he is allergic to blood.

Afterward, I secretly began to slurp books in my father's bookstore. Life was terribly lonely until I met Carmilla, Draculink's beautiful niece.

Now life is great. Carmilla and her uncle moved out of their cemetery and into the basement of the Library of the World. That's where we discovered Dracuville, the city of ink drinkers.

Carmilla is the ink-drinking love of my life. Together we slurp up big, thrilling books with a twin straw. As the ink makes its way up into our straw, and from there into our stomachs, the pages turn white. We constantly crave new books, but since we live below the biggest library in the world, that's not a problem. Uncle Draculink thinks we're complete gluttons.

Right now we are drinking a

huge book of fairy tales. Carmilla chose it. She's bored with adventure stories. But fairy tales aren't really my cup of tea. I prefer more action.

"So which tale are we going to swallow next?" Carmilla asked, her eyes sparkling.

"Well, I don't know. 'The Three Little Pigs,' maybe . . . or how about 'Ali Baba and the Forty Thieves'?"

"No, we already got a taste of those. I'd rather try 'Cinderella,' 'Sleeping Beauty,' or 'Snow White.'"

I laughed stupidly. "Right, all those stories are filled with Prince Charmings!"

"And so what? There's more to

life than just battles and adventures. Feelings and love count too!"

I knew that. But I go for real love stories, like the one I'm living with Carmilla.

"How about reading a tale with a little more action?" I suggested.

"Such as?"

I pretended to ponder the question, but I already had a clear idea.

"I don't know, maybe a story with an ogre, a witch, or a wolf," I said.

"But there's a witch in 'Snow White' and in 'Sleeping Beauty'!" Carmilla pointed out.

"What a joke!" I said. "That witch is actually a queen, and a fool, too. She just ends up getting trapped by dwarfs!"

Carmilla sighed. I knew what she was thinking: *Boys are dumb.* And I am a boy. . . .

4

"Okay, then, what's your great idea?" she asked impatiently.

"Well, there's a tale that scares me every time—" I began.

"Tell me!"

I was thinking of "Bluebeard," but at the last second I changed my mind without knowing why.

"It's—it's 'Little Red Riding Hood,'" I said.

Carmilla had a good laugh. It so happened that "Little Red Riding Hood" was one of her favorite stories, and it didn't even have a Prince Charming.

"It has a girl hero," my girlfriend reminded me.

"Not true. The wolf is the hero. And he's a boy!"

We went on teasing each other for a while, but then we planted our straw on page one and started drinking the tale: "Once upon a time, a little girl, the prettiest of all in the village . . ."

two

Sipped by a Book . . .

Right after the first paragraph, I tried to drink the picture of the wolf that was on the left page. Carmilla tried to do the same. We were both sipping vigorously when something unbelievable occurred. Suddenly we started shrinking, like in *Alice's Adventures*

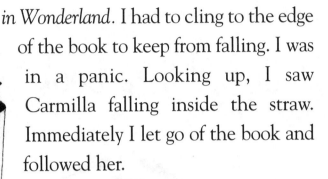

in Wonderland. I had to cling to the edge of the book to keep from falling. I was in a panic. Looking up, I saw Carmilla falling inside the straw. Immediately I let go of the book and followed her.

An overpowering force pulled us down . . . down . . . down the plastic tube—until we landed hard, bottoms up, noses to the ground. Stunned and covered with dust, we managed to get to our feet.

We were in the middle of a huge forest, as lost as Tom Thumb or Hansel and Gretel.

"What just happened?" Carmilla asked. She seemed awed by the beauty of the giant trees.

"I think the book drank us up. Or the tale did."

"Wrong!" a powerful voice roared. "I am the one who inhaled you here!"

I turned around. A wolf was facing me—the wolf from the story!

"By what right? *We* are the ink drinkers!" I said, pointing to Carmilla and me.

"Then who are the drinkers of ink drinkers?" the wolf howled as he jumped up and down excitedly around us.

"Well, that would be us!" said a little female voice.

It was Little Red Riding Hood! Nearly everyone from the story was there!

Carmilla pulled at my sleeve. She looked pale and frightened.

"How are we going to get out of the book?" she said. "Do you see the tip of our straw anywhere, Odilon?"

"I don't have a clue. But let's try to negotiate with these two. Maybe they know the way out."

The wolf was watching us, his teeth bared in a snarl and an ominous gurgling coming from his throat. As for Little Red Riding Hood, the little brat was staring at us with undisguised contempt.

"The wolf and I, we get tired of living out the same old story," she said. "So we've decided to take your straw and escape to fresher air."

"What if I simply eat them alive?" the wolf suggested, salivating.

"Be quiet, Wolf!" replied Little Red Riding Hood as she gave him a tap on the muzzle.

"Did you by chance forget that to get out of the book, we need to find two replacements?"

The wolf started whining. Little Red Riding Hood turned back to us.

"You are about to take our places and live our story. Meanwhile, Wolf and I will explore your world and do whatever pleases us. Ah, the joy of freedom!"

As Little Red Riding Hood uttered these words, our straw suddenly appeared out of nowhere.

"You can't do such a thing!" I said in a rage. "You're imaginary characters. You don't really exist!"

Giggling, the beast and the little girl jumped into our twin straw. I leaped toward them, but in vain. They were gone!

When I looked again toward Carmilla, she

too had disappeared. Little Red Riding Hood had somehow returned.

I got threateningly close to her and growled, "Stop playing games, little pest!"

Scared, Little Red Riding Hood took a step back.

"But—but I'm not who you believe me to be! I'm—I'm Carmilla!"

That's when I looked at my paws and let out a long, grim howl.

three

A Mouthwatering Smell of Fresh Meat

Never had we experienced anything so horrible. Not only was our predicament ridiculous, it was also dangerous. What if we were to remain prisoners of this tale? What if we had to relive the story to its final page?

"Odilon!"

"Yes."

"Do you remember how the story ends?"

"Of course! The wolf devours everyone."

Carmilla burst into loud sobs. I didn't know what to do to console her. I took her in my paws, careful not to scratch her.

"Don't despair. We'll get out of this mess," I said.

"I'm not so sure. Don't forget: I am Little Red Riding Hood and you are the wolf."

My ears drooped as I understood what she meant. I would eventually eat Carmilla!

"We can't live out such a story!" I shouted. "It's not possible!"

"I don't think we have a choice."

"But I can't just wolf you down."

Carmilla gently escaped from my hug and dried her tears.

"If it were only that! Don't you remember what happens next?"

This time I had to think a bit.

"Wait a minute," I finally said. "There are several possible endings. Either I eat you . . ."

Suddenly Carmilla/Little Red Riding Hood grimaced with unmistakable disgust.

"Or a hunter kills the wolf, slices open its belly, and saves everyone," she said.

"Oops!"

I howled like a dying wolf at the prospect of such a ghastly ordeal.

"Which version is in our book?" I asked in alarm.

Carmilla shook her head. "I don't remember."

"Oh, no!"

We had definitely stumbled into a vicious trap.

"I have an idea, Little Red Carmilla. Since we have no choice, we'll go along with the story. But in our own way. Take your basket and follow me."

Carmilla grabbed the basket, in which lay a cake and a little pot of butter. Then we set out through the woods.

"Where are we headed?" Carmilla asked.

"To Grandma's, of course! Maybe she'll be kinder than the others and offer us some good advice."

It was a long walk, much longer than I would have thought.

"Are you sure we're going in the right direction?"

"Listen, Carmilla, are you forgetting what

kind of beast I am? A wolf's sense of smell is infallible!"

As I said these words, I felt every hair on my furry body bristle. Indeed, my sense of smell was alerting me to the fact that my girlfriend could easily become a succulent and juicy roast. Horrified by my own appetite and my eagerness to swallow her, I stepped up the pace.

"Wait for me!" she begged. "You have four legs. I only have two, and short ones at that!"

After a while the path widened and we arrived at the threshold of the forest. A mouthwatering smell of fresh meat was emanating from Carmilla.

"Look, there's a house over there!" she shouted.

"Yes, that's where we're going," I said, suddenly bursting into laughter.

"What's so funny?" my girlfriend asked.

"I'm such a fool! Instead of taking the shortcut, we followed the longest path, the very one the wolf suggests to Little Red Riding Hood in the tale."

Carmilla seemed bewildered. She looked so pretty—pretty enough to sink my teeth into!

"And it's only now you realize that?" she said.

Her cheeks grew pink with anger. I quickly turned my eyes away from her.

"Come, Grandma is waiting for us."

four

Odilon, a Wolf for Real

It was a house made of stone, with tiny windows and a roof of slate. I knocked at the door. We heard a weak voice.

"Who is it?"

I whispered into Carmilla's ear. "It would be better if you answered."

"Uh, it's your granddaughter, Little Car—Little Red Riding Hood," she stammered. "My mother sent me to bring you a cake and a little pot of butter."

"Lift the latch and push open the door."

Upon hearing these lovely words, which meant so much to the wolf I had become, I couldn't help licking my lips.

We entered. It was dark inside. At the other end of the room a very old lady was curled up in her bed. A nightcap adorned with a ribbon covered her head. She didn't seem to be well.

"I get the impression you're not alone, my little girl."

Carmilla hesitated before replying. "Indeed, Odiwolf is with me."

"Who is that?"

"The wolf!"

Grandma's body shook as she heard these words.

"But—but he was supposed to arrive first and eat me. Why have you changed the story?" said Grandma with indignation in her voice.

"Very simple, Grandma: Little Red Riding Hood I am not, and the wolf he is not!"

"I don't understand. I don't see an ounce of difference between Little Red Riding Hood and you, or between him and the wolf!"

Carmilla tried to explain, but Grandma would not budge.

"The wolf is supposed to eat me up, period.

Then he'll swallow you! You're a character in a book, so just comply with the story!"

"I am not a character in this book!" Carmilla shouted.

"I don't care. And you over there, eat me up or go away!"

If I had had a choice, I would've gone home at once. I was getting fed up with this tale.

"Stand back, Carmilla. I'll devour her so that she leaves us alone. Anyway, let's not forget that in the story, the wolf hasn't eaten in at least three days."

"No, this is a trap. If you eat her up, you'll become a prisoner of the story and have to eat me as well. We'll be stuck inside these pages forever. Is that what you want?"

I started whining. "I don't know what I

want anymore, except that I am starving and that your flesh is surely tasty."

Flabbergasted, Carmilla fainted. I approached her, driven by an irresistible need to bite into her. After all, I was the wolf—and I had two full rows of fangs!

I couldn't resist the temptation any longer. . . .

five

An Out-of-the-Ordinary Grandma

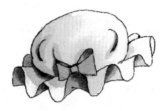

"**O**dilon, don't do it, my little one. You'll regret it forever."

"Mind your own business, Grandma! You'll be next anyway."

I brought my face close to Carmilla's. The sweet scent of her skin was irresistible.

Then, suddenly, I froze. How on earth had Grandma guessed my name? Turning my eyes toward the bed, I noticed that the old woman was sitting up and had removed her nightcap. The face was vaguely familiar, but it was too dark to see the features clearly.

And then somehow the words of the tale spontaneously came out of my mouth.

"Grandma, your arms are so long!" I said.

"The better to reach the highest books, my child."

"Grandma, your legs are so long! But why are they flabby?"

"Because I don't need them anymore. Nowadays I float, my child."

"Grandma, your ears are so ridiculously small!"

"Once upon a time, they were beautiful. Now I'm getting hard of hearing, my child."

"Grandma, your eyes are so red!"

"The better to see at night, my child."

"Grandma, your teeth are so big, so bright, and so sharp!"

"These are the teeth of an ink drinker, kid!"

Suddenly Grandma's strange answers made sense. Grandma was Uncle Draculink! And to think that I had almost devoured him . . .

At that moment, I felt my claws retracting, my fangs reverting to teeth, and my fur disappearing. I stood up on my feet. Back to normal at last!

I was again in front of the Library of the World. Carmilla, still unconscious and still

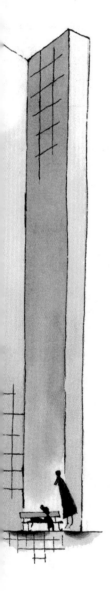

looking like Little Red Riding Hood, was lying on our favorite bench.

"Uncle Draculink, I was about to make a huge blunder."

"I know. When I saw the wolf and Little Red Riding Hood in Dracuville, I knew something was very wrong. So I entered the story, sent Grandma on a little vacation, and took her place to see how you and Carmilla were getting on. You know, it's not uncommon for an ink drinker with a hearty appetite to get sucked into a book. In order not to remain a prisoner within the pages, you have to overcome the story and modify some of the details."

If, that morning, Uncle Draculink

had warned us that we might land at the other end of the straw, we would never have believed him.

"By the way, Uncle, where are they?"

"Whom do you mean?"

"Little Red Riding Hood and the wolf, of course!"

"They, as well as Grandma, are back in the tale. You might say that order has been restored." He pointed to my girlfriend clad in red. "How about taking care of her?"

I leaned over the motionless body of my Little Red Carmilla. How was I going to awaken her gently?

This brought to mind the story of Sleeping Beauty. Easy as pie! Smiling, I knelt down so as to drop on Carmilla's lips a long and tender kiss with a taste reminiscent of the

blue ink from the southern seas. Her pretty eyes opened.

As soon as she saw me, she recovered the appearance of an ink drinker. Then she yawned.

"Oh, I feel as if I've slept for a hundred years," she said, although she'd been unconscious no longer than five minutes. Ah, the magic of fairy tales!

"And do you remember who I am?" I asked.

"Of course, you're Odilon, my Prince Charming!"

About the Author

ÉRIC SANVOISIN is one bizarre writer. Using a straw, he loves to suck the ink from all the fan letters he receives. That's what inspired him to write this story. He's sure that just as there are blood brothers and blood sisters, everyone who reads this book will become his ink brother or sister. If you write to him, he will send you a straw. That's a promise, or else he won't be writing again anytime soon.

About the Illustrator

If there's one thing MARTIN MATJE hates to do, it's write his biography. Biographies are just never much fun. So forget big dictionaries, this is one bio that's close to zero!